The Enormous Turnip

illustrated by Cristiana Cerretti

Child's Play (International) Ltd
Ashworth Rd, Bridgemead, Swindon, SN5 7YD UK

There was once a lovely garden, belonging to an old couple, which was filled with the most splendid flowers, vegetables and fruit.

"What's the secret?" their friends used to ask.
"Why don't our plants grow as tall?"

The couple used to smile and say nothing. There was no secret. They tilled the ground thoroughly, and they planted their seeds with care.

They fed and watered their plants
as though they were their own children.
And they talked to them and sang to them
to make sure they were happy.

One Spring morning, the two of them
were in the garden, admiring their crops.

"It's going to be a good year,"
observed the old woman.

"Everything looks very special," agreed the man. "And just look at that turnip!"

"The best!" she nodded. "Boiled and mashed with pepper and butter!"

Everything they planted that year grew better than ever before. The potatoes were as big as footballs, and the tomatoes were firm and juicy. The bean plants were overloaded with beans. The man was especially proud of their deep red roses. He could not remember a better year.

But the biggest thing
of all was the turnip.

The turnip leaves alone
made a small forest, and
the village children loved
to play hide and seek in it.

The day came when the old woman could
not wait any longer to taste the turnip.
She took a firm hold of its green top.
She pulled and pulled, but it did not budge.

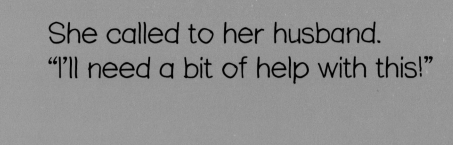

She called to her husband.
"I'll need a bit of help with this!"

The man came
over and took hold
of her waist. They
both pulled and pulled,
but the turnip did not
budge one inch.

They called out to their
granddaughter to help.
All three pulled and pulled,
but the turnip did not
budge one inch.

"I know!" said the granddaughter.
"Let's ask the dog to help!"

The dog ran over and grabbed hold of
the girl's waist. All four pulled and pulled,
but the turnip did not budge one inch.
"The cat's doing nothing," said the dog.
"Let's ask it to help!"

The cat was perfectly
happy to carry on lying
in the sun, but at last
it agreed to help.

It took firm hold
of the dog's waist,
and they all pulled as
hard as they could.
But the turnip did
not budge one inch.

"I'm sorry," said the old man to his wife.
"You'll have to do without turnip tonight.
We'll just have to leave it in the ground.
What a waste!"

"Wait a minute," said the cat.
"Let's ask the mouse to help."
"Don't be silly!" laughed the dog.
"Whoever heard of a mouse pulling up a turnip?"

"Every little helps," observed the old man, and called for the mouse to come and help them pull. The mouse grabbed hold of the cat and pulled with all his might. But the turnip did not budge one inch. They all pulled again, and again and again.

"Well done, Mouse!" called out the old woman. "I felt it move! Pull, everyone, pull!"

They all heaved one last time,
and with a great noise and tumble...

...the turnip shot out of the ground.

It took hours to wash and chop and cook the turnip. Some was roasted, and some was boiled and mashed.

Everyone agreed it was the best turnip they had ever tasted, and there was enough to feed the whole village for a month.

And the old couple still had plenty
of turnip seeds for next year!